Listen, MY BRIDGE is SO COOL!

The Story of THE THREE BILLY GOATS GRUFF as Told by THE TROLL

by Nancy Loewen

illustrated by Cristian Bernardini

PICTURE WINDOW BOOKS
a capstone imprint

Editor: Jill Kalz
Designer: Lori Bye
Premedia Specialist: Tori Abraham
The illustrations in this book were created digitally.

o-ö♋x♋ö-o

Picture Window Books
1710 Roe Crest Drive
North Mankato, MN 56003
www.mycapstone.com

Library of Congress Cataloging-in-Publication Data
Names: Loewen, Nancy, 1964– author. |
Bernardini, Cristian, 1975– illustrator.
Title: Listen, my bridge is so cool! : the story of the three billy goats Gruff as
told by the troll / by Nancy Loewen ; illustrated by Cristian Bernardini.
Description: North Mankato, Minnesota : Picture Window Books, a Capstone
imprint, [2018] | Series: The other side of the story | Summary: In this
humorous adaptation of the tale, Arty the troll is really a poetry-loving, non-
aggressive guy who is being pressured by the Troll Patrol to act more troll-
like or lose his rights to the bridge — so he makes a deal with the largest of
the billy goats that makes them both look good.
Identifiers: LCCN 2017039789 (print) | LCCN 2017042741 (eBook) |
ISBN 9781515823018 (eBook PDF) | ISBN 9781515822974 (library binding) |
ISBN 9781515823179 (paperback)
Subjects: LCSH: Asbjørnsen, Peter Christen, 1812–1885. Tre bukkene Bruse—
Adaptations. | Fairy tales. | Trolls—Juvenile fiction. | Goats—Juvenile
fiction. | Humorous stories. | CYAC: Fairy tales. | Trolls—Fiction. | Goats—
Fiction. | Humorous stories. | LCGFT: Humorous fiction.
Classification: LCC PZ8.L837 (eBook) | LCC PZ8.L837 Li 2018 (print) |
DDC [E]—dc23
LC record available at https://lccn.loc.gov/2017039789

Printed and bound in the United States of America.
010847S18

Hello! My name is Arty. I'm the troll in that famous story about the goats. You know, the one with all the trip-trapping across a bridge.

Are you surprised to see me? Did you think I was done for when the biggest goat kicked me off the bridge?

Here, have some homemade bread and jam. (It's wild strawberry.)
Settle back, and I'll tell you the REAL story.

I've never been like other trolls.

In Troll School, I got good grades — which meant I was the worst in my class. (Trolls aren't supposed to be smart.) Instead of practicing roars and chest-thumping, I made art and baked pies.

I wasn't big and clumsy. I didn't even smell bad!

"Are you sure you're a troll?" the other students teased. "Maybe you're an elf!"

When we finished school, the Troll Placement Board gave us jobs. I was to guard a little bridge in the middle of nowhere. The other trolls laughed. But to me, the job was perfect.

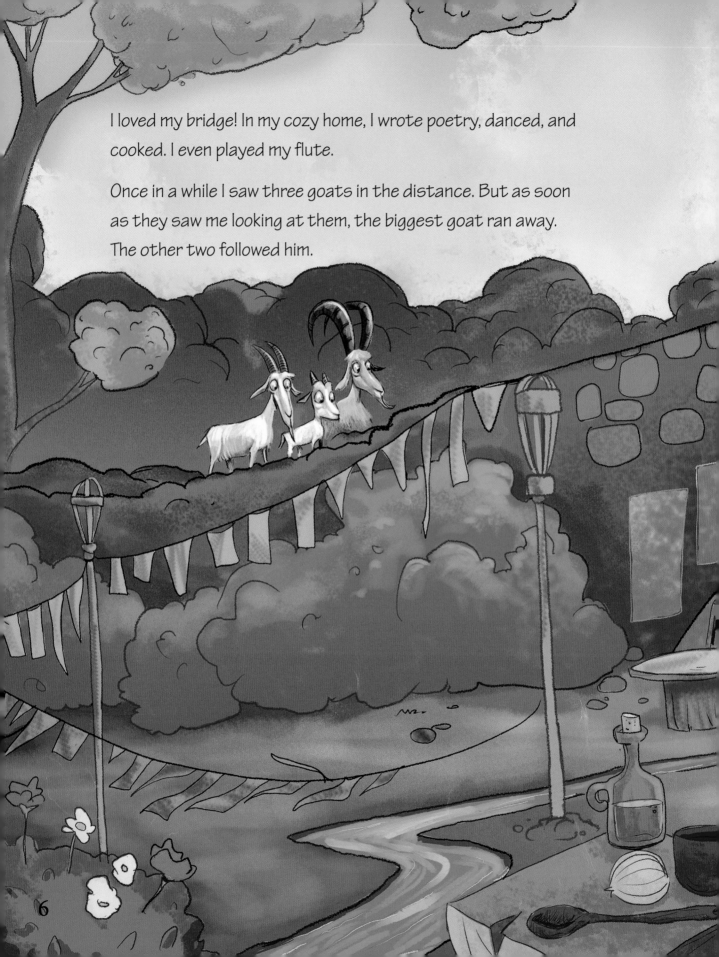

I loved my bridge! In my cozy home, I wrote poetry, danced, and cooked. I even played my flute.

Once in a while I saw three goats in the distance. But as soon as they saw me looking at them, the biggest goat ran away. The other two followed him.

One day a crow dropped a letter on my head.

8

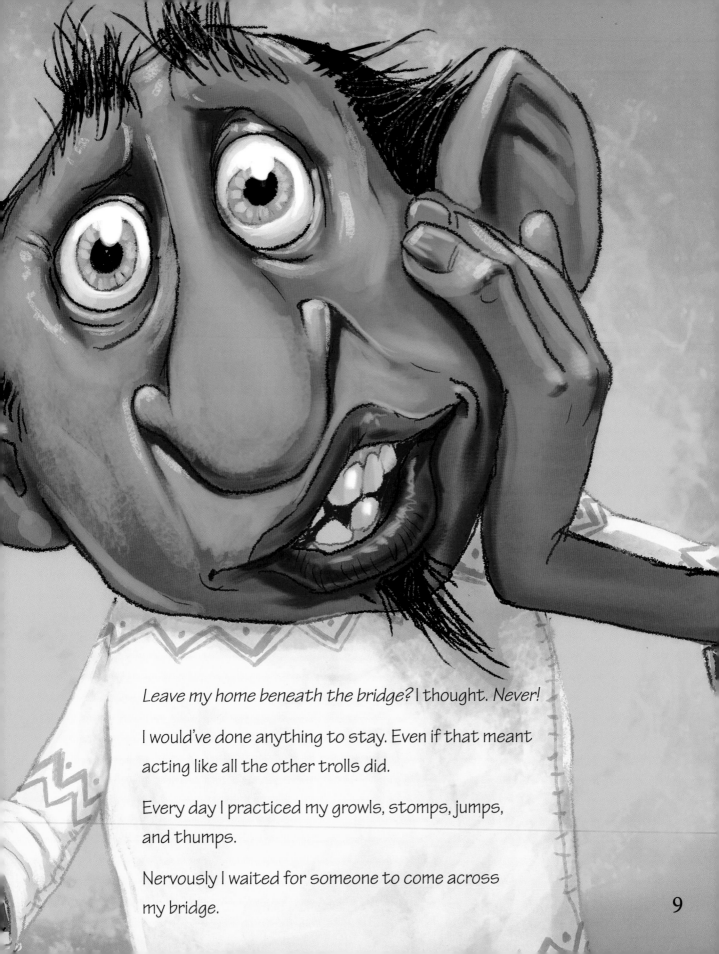

Leave my home beneath the bridge? I thought. Never!

I would've done anything to stay. Even if that meant acting like all the other trolls did.

Every day I practiced my growls, stomps, jumps, and thumps.

Nervously I waited for someone to come across my bridge.

9

Finally, my chance came. It was a beautiful summer day. I was just about to make a batch of my world-class fish stew when I heard a clicking overhead.

TRIP-TRAP, TRIP-TRAP

This was it!

I hopped atop the bridge and said, "WHO'S TRIPPING ACROSS MY BRIDGE?"

A little goat looked at me curiously. "*You're* the troll?" he said. "Huh. OK."

"Yes!" I hollered. "And I'm going to GOBBLE YOU UP!"

"Oh, you don't want to eat *me*," the little goat said. "Wait for my brother. He's much bigger. He'll come along soon."

"Fine!" I said, and the goat trotted off with a grin.

11

Back beneath the bridge, I calmed myself with a few sips of pine needle tea. Pretty soon I heard **TRIP-TRAP, TRIP-TRAP.**

I scrambled onto the bridge and tried again.
"WHO'S TRIPPING ACROSS MY BRIDGE?" I yelled.

This goat was bigger than the first. He didn't seem scared either. "Oh, hey!" he said. "We just want to graze in that awesome patch of grass over there. Are you cool with that?"

"Sure, that's —," I started to say, then caught myself. "I mean, **I'M GOING TO GOBBLE YOU UP!"**

"Um, maybe you could wait for my big brother?" the goat said. "The guy is huge."

"Fine!" I waved the goat off.

Before I could refresh my tea ...

TRIP-TRAP! TRIP-TRAP!

For the third time I pulled myself onto the bridge.

"WHO'S THAT TRAMPING ACROSS MY BRIDGE?"

I said to the biggest goat I'd ever seen. I thumped my chest. "I'm going to **GOBBLE YOU UP** ... like, **RIGHT NOW!** ... Yep, that's exactly what I'm going to do! Gobble. You. **UP!** Just watch me!"

The big goat stood in front of me, trembling.

"Wait a minute," I said. "Are you really scared?"

He nodded.

"Me too," I confessed in a rush. "I don't want to hurt anyone, really.
But the Troll Patrol says I have to either act like a troll or move.
And I really love my bridge."

The goat continued to stare at me. "I might be big," he whispered, "but I'm not brave."

"Do your brothers tease you?" I asked.

"Sometimes," he admitted.

"They didn't think you would actually come to the bridge, did they?" I said.

He shook his head.

"But you DID," I told him. "You were scared, and you came here anyway. So you really ARE brave."

"I am?" he asked.

"Yes!" I said.

Oh, this couldn't have worked out better.

"Let's give them all a good show," I said. "We'll just *pretend* to fight. Your brothers will change their minds about you. And the Troll Patrol will change its mind about me!"

19

And that's just what we did.

These days, my life under the bridge is better than ever. Every so often, Big Bad Billy and I put on a huge pretend fight. It's making him feel better about himself. My troll skills must be improving too. I haven't gotten any more letters from the Troll Patrol.

Now, how about some more bread and jam?

Think About It

Describe how the troll, Arty, is different from other trolls. Use the illustrations in the book to support your answer.

What were your thoughts when you saw the biggest goat for the first time? How did you expect him to act? How was the character different from what you expected?

This story is told from the point of view of the troll. If the biggest goat were telling this story, what details would change?

Look online to find a traditional telling of "The Three Billy Goats Gruff" story. How is this version of the story the same? How is it different?

Glossary

character—a person, animal, or creature in a story
point of view—a way of looking at something
version—an account of something from a certain point of view

Read More

Hu-Van Wright, Rebecca, retold by. *The Three Billy Goats Gruff.* Cambridge, Mass.: Star Bright Books, 2014.

Pinkney, Jerry. *The Three Billy Goats Gruff.* New York; Boston: Little, Brown and Company, 2017.

Shaskan, Stephen. *The Three Triceratops Tuff.* New York: Beach Lane Books, 2013.

Internet Sites

Use FactHound to find Internet sites related to this book.

Visit *www.facthound.com*

Just type in 9781515822974 and go.

Look for all the books in the series:

Believe Me, Goldilocks Rocks!

Believe Me, I Never Felt a Pea!

For Real, I Paraded in My Underpants!

Frankly, I'd Rather Spin Myself a New Name!

Frankly, I Never Wanted to Kiss Anybody!

Honestly, Our Music Stole the Show!

Honestly, Red Riding Hood Was Rotten!

Listen, My Bridge Is SO Cool!

No Kidding, Mermaids Are a Joke!

No Lie, I Acted Like a Beast!

No Lie, Pigs (and Their Houses) CAN Fly!

Really, Rapunzel Needed a Haircut!

Seriously, Cinderella Is SO Annoying!

Seriously, Snow White Was SO Forgetful!

Truly, We Both Loved Beauty Dearly!

Trust Me, Hansel and Gretel Are SWEET!

Trust Me, Jack's Beanstalk Stinks!

Truthfully, Something Smelled Fishy!

Super-cool stuff!

Check out projects, games and lots more at
www.capstonekids.com